# White Star

by Rebecca Wilson

The Young Writers Series

Published by:
The Benchmark Group LLC
148 Del Crest Drive Suite One
Nashville, TN 37217-4640
BenchmarkGroup1@aol.com

*The integrity of the upright will guide them.* Proverbs 11:3a

in association with:
McDougal Publishing
P.O. Box 3595
Hagerstown, MD 21742-3595
www.mcdougalpublishing.com

ISBN 978-1-58158-106-5

Printed in the United States of America
For Worldwide Distribution

I dedicate this story to my parents. Thanks, dad and mom, for believing in me. Thanks for everything!!!!!

*Rebecca*

# Prologue

*I write this to no one in particular simply because I have no one but myself. My father has denounced me from my vast inheritance because he believes I am to blame for my dear mum's death. I have no brothers and only one sister whom I am hardly ever pleasured to see since she is wed and has a husband and children to attend.*

*That is why I have left London for good and have taken a most prestigious job with White Star Line. Out of my 18 years, I now dedicate my life to the ocean and voyaging on ships.*

*My only dear possession is my grandfather's violin, which I sorrowfully do not know how to play but simply transport from place to place in its case. I keep it safe underneath my berth where no one will see it.*

*As I stand on the deck of my first ship where passengers are preparing to board, I stare intently at the distant emerald-green hills of bewitching Ireland. I am the most excited, yet the most forlorn, I have been since my mum passed away. On my first ship voyage as a steward with White Star Line, I am utterly alone. I have no friends, not even one person to* address this letter to. So I will simply drop this letter down into the blue chambers of the ocean and let the water have it.

To whoever may be reading,
Damon Ledger

*1*

Daphne Palmer breathed deeply the cool, yet heavy April air as she peddled her bike down the sidewalk. It was late Thursday afternoon. By the way the morning and early afternoon had just dragged by, Daphne could already see that the remainder of the day would be just as dismal. School had been terrible, and the bag of school books on her back were like weights constantly reminding her of her melancholy life.

She replayed the embarrassment she had endured that day when she slipped in the cafeteria and dropped her food tray. Only one person stopped to help her—Ivan, the strange nerd no one talked to. Ivan was a loner, but if it bothered him, he didn't reveal it. Daphne had always tried to avoid him, knowing that any chance of her moving up in school social circles wouldn't be helped by talking to him.

"Are you alright?" Ivan had asked her.

Daphne, pretending to be too busy gathering everything back on her plastic tray, didn't respond.

She could hear the passing cheerleaders snicker at her. All Daphne wanted was for Ivan to go away. She hurried to a table where some other new students were sitting. From the corner of her eye, Daphne saw Ivan sitting at a table alone.

Frustrated, Daphne wiped the relentless image of Ivan away from her mind as she coasted down the sidewalk. Two boys playing war in their front yard said something and laughed as she passed by. Daphne could only imagine what they were saying: "Hey look, there goes that weird new kid!"

That was her problem. Daphne was lonely. She had absolutely no friends.

She was new in Atlanta. She and her father had moved here more than five months ago, and yet Daphne had nobody. She just had her dad, but sometimes he was so busy with work and the situations around him that Daphne felt like she was in the background. Thinking of her mother pained her. It had been exactly two years since her mother had died of leukemia. It was because of the unrelenting memory of her mother that her dad had taken on a new job and they had moved from Florida to Georgia. In Florida with her mother and father, everything had been practically perfect. They lived only minutes from the ocean and, almost every day, Daphne and her mother would ride bikes to the beach and just spend time with each other. On weekends, her dad would join them and they would add to their ever-growing collection of seashells and large jar of black shark teeth.

Daphne sighed, shaking the aching memories and images from her mind as she felt a cold raindrop fall on her bare arm. With thunder rumbling across the darkening sky above her, she turned the last corner and started to peddle the slight incline.

Her new school was nice enough, she supposed, but it was big and Daphne felt lost within the crowd. There were too many cliques, even if they were small groups, and she couldn't break through. It was the same problem with her new drama club. Nobody around here seemed to want a newcomer.

Her house came into view and she saw that her father was not home yet. Her heart sank as she pulled in the driveway. The empty house was dark. It made Daphne shiver.

She hopped off her bike and started to walk it into the garage when she noticed her neighbor, Mrs. Smith, kneeling in her flower garden pulling weeds.

"Hello, Mrs. Smith," Daphne said as she knocked her kickstand out to prop up her bike.

Mrs. Smith looked up, her jeans soiled with dirt and on her head her favorite wide-brimmed straw hat decorated with pins from the Olympics that had come to Atlanta in 1996.

"Why hello, Daphne," Mrs. Smith smiled, her tan face lined with age. "How was school?"

"It was good," Daphne lied as she closed the garage door. "Your garden looks great." She glanced at her plain front yard and then at Mrs. Smith's elaborate, colorful one. Mrs. Smith had won the Yard of the Month award twice recently.

"Thank you," Mrs. Smith said as she stood to her feet and pulled off her garden gloves. "It sounds like a thunderstorm is moving in. My flowers need the rain."

The two glanced up at the sky. Rain was slowly beginning to fall.

"You play the violin, don't you Daphne?" Mrs. Smith suddenly asked.

"Yes ma'am," Daphne replied slowly, hoping Mrs. Smith wasn't about to ask her to perform for anything.

"Good, because there's something I want to give you. Follow me into the house," Mrs. Smith turned and the young girl followed. The wiry, short woman led her on the stone path to the back door. Daphne felt that at least she had one friend, even if she was an elderly lady.

Inside it was cool and smelled like lavender. The only sounds came from the grandfather clock in the corner of the den and the calico cat curled up on the leather chair. Daphne stopped to stroke the cat as Mrs. Smith went down the hall.

While she waited for Mrs. Smith to return, Daphne admired the room. Most of the things were antiques, from the clock to the delicate lamps to the little small table centered on a vibrant rug.

Finally, Mrs. Smith returned. In her arms was an old, beat-up violin case.

"My husband James loved antiques, as you can see," Mrs. Smith said as she placed the hard case on the couch. "Before he died he told me what to get rid of and what to keep. As for this old violin, he told me to give it away if I ever encountered a talented violinist. It's very old and weather-beaten, but it's quite valuable."

Daphne watched with wonder as Mrs. Smith raised the lid on the case. The hinges creaked and seemed a bit wobbly. It was obvious that the case had taken a few bumps and knocks.

Inside, lying snugly in a thick lining of red velvet was a very old violin.

Daphne ran her fingers gently over the roughened wood that once, long ago, had been smooth and sleek. The black bridge had a crack and the strings were stiff and completely out of tune, but there was something about the violin that beckoned to her. It seemed as if it had a past and had gone through a life of mystery. Daphne was greatly intrigued by it.

"It looks as if it has gotten wet at some point," Daphne commented softly, noticing the ridges that had destroyed the wooden instrument.

"Yes. I think my husband told me it was crafted in the late 1800s, so there's no telling what it has gone through," Mrs. Smith said.

"Thank you so much," Daphne said as she shut the case. She smiled at Mrs. Smith. "Thank you for thinking of me. I feel honored."

"Oh, you deserve it," Mrs. Smith returned the smile. "Now, how about some milk and cookies?"

✦

That night, after she had breezed through her homework, Daphne sat on her bed with the violin case and opened it carefully as if it might break beneath her hands. The inside of the case had a funny, musty smell. It almost had the scent of salt from the ocean, evoking Daphne's memory of living by the beach. Shaking her head at her foolishness, she ignored the odor. Picking up the delicate violin, she held it firmly.

Yes, it had been through some brutal weather, but it was a gorgeous piece of work nevertheless. The bow was missing, Daphne discovered with disappointment. She wouldn't have been able to play it anyhow in its condition, but still, a violin felt somewhat lost without its companion, the bow. She continued admiring her new possession, plucking the strings curiously only to frown at the flatness of the sound.

Then a corner of white paper caught her eye. It was folded into a hidden pouch in the lower corner of the case.

Daphne stared at it for a moment, wondering what it could be. A sheet of old music perhaps? A letter of authenticity? Setting down the violin, she tugged the paper free from its pouch.

It was a very old envelope.

Holding her breath, Daphne opened it and pulled out a sheet of paper. It too was stained but over the paper's face was the nicest penmanship Daphne had seen in a while.

It started:

*Thursday, April 11, 1912*
DOCKED AT QUEENSTOWN, IRELAND
*I write this to no one in particular simply because I have no one but myself. My father has denounced me from my vast inheritance because he believes I am to blame for my dear mum's death. I have no brothers and only one sister …"*

Daphne's eyes raced across the paper. It was signed "Damon Ledger."

She set it down with a trembling hand. Her heart was pounding. Then she read it again.

"Thursday, April 11, 1912…" Daphne glanced up

at her calendar. Today was April 11, 2002. Her eyes widened in a strange terror as she hastily calculated the distance of time that lay between the two separate years. The letter was exactly 90 years old today.

So the violin had belonged to a Mr. Damon Ledger who was originally from London and at 18 had joined White Star Line as a steward on ships.

Something about the letter scared Daphne and yet deeply pleased her. Was it because the author was just as lonely and friendless as Daphne? She hadn't lost her entire inheritance, but she had lost her mother just as he had...

She packed the violin away but kept the case on her bed, then read the letter once more with disbelieving eyes. Now her imagination was set on fire. An idea came to her mind and she got a sheet of notebook paper and a pen.

Sitting at her desk, Daphne stared at the blank sheet of paper that was lying before her. Then she gazed longingly at the 90-year-old letter.

I thought he said he was going to throw the letter into the ocean, Daphne thought. Why was it in the case? Why hadn't Mr. Smith noticed the letter when he had purchased the violin? Or why didn't I notice it when Mrs. Smith opened the case? I don't remember seeing it in there then. Her thoughts ceased abruptly when she heard a knocking on her door.

"Daph? You awake?"

It was her father.

Quickly covering up the old letter, Daphne called him in.

Her father looked tired. He was already dressed for bed and there were dark rings about his droopy eyes.

"Working on homework?" He asked placing a hand on Daphne's shoulder.

Daphne nodded. "You look tired, Dad. Is something wrong?"

"No," he smiled wearily. "Just Atlanta traffic, I'm still trying to get used to it."

She nodded again and picked up her pen.

"Well, I'll let you get to work. Sorry I was late coming home today," he said and dropped a kiss on her head. "I think I'll order a pizza for supper."

"That's fine with me," Daphne replied.

"Alright, I'll call you when it gets here," her father said and quietly shut the door.

Daphne immediately took out the letter.

She read it one last time, and then took in a deep breath.

She began to write:

*Thursday, April 11, 2002*

*Dear Mr. Ledger,*

*I don't know why I'm writing you since, if you were still alive, you'd be 111 years old, but my neighbor gave me this antique violin and case, which I'm supposing belonged to you. I found your letter in there: the one where you mention you've just joined White Star Line (whatever that is) and are going to be a steward aboard some fancy ship. Don't worry. Your grandfather's violin is still in one piece, although it is looking on the rough side. I promise I'll take care of it, and you really have no need to worry because I have a violin of my own and have been playing since I was five.*

*I understand your loneliness because I feel it too more than ever right now. I just moved to Atlanta and cannot make any friends. That's pretty much why I'm writing you. You need a friend and so do I.*

*Write back if you can, even if you are 111. My address is on the envelope.*

*Sincerely,*

*Daphne Palmer*

Content with what she had written, Daphne sighed. She re-read it and found no mistakes, so she took an envelope, folded the letter, and put it inside. On the front, she scribbled "To Damon Ledger" and on the back she wrote her address. Then a thought struck her. How would she mail this to him?

Shrugging and telling herself the letter she had written was just for fun, Daphne stuck it in the violin case where she could deal with it later and slid the case under her bed. She joined her dad in the living room, forgetting about the letter and Damon Ledger.

# 2

The waves crashed onto the sand, washing white foam and broken chips of shells up to the beach. Daphne and her mother were walking barefoot along the beach with their two pails, examining shells that came to shore.

"Look at this, Daph," her mother called, and Daphne turned around to see the huge starfish she was holding up.

"It's missing an arm," Daphne said, and took it from her mom to examine it.

"It'll grow back," Mrs. Palmer smiled. "Sometimes the broken misfits stay closer to our hearts than a perfect, spotless one would."

"But why?" Daphne asked as a wave crested and washed foam around their ankles.

"Because they need love more."

Her mother's words echoed in Daphne's mind. Handing the starfish back, Daphne turned to go on with her own searching. The wind was suddenly cold as dark clouds blocked the sun. The waves grew rougher, crashing and turning, full of gray wrath. That was when Daphne saw it.

*She had wandered far it seemed, and was about to turn back when she saw an object ride on the crest of an incoming wave. The wave dispersed at her feet, washing something ashore. It was the violin case.*

*Daphne gasped and bent to pick it up.*

*There were more dents and bumps on the case than she remembered.*

*Smiling, Daphne turned to call her mother to see the great find.*

*But when she turned, her mother was gone. Daphne was completely alone on the stormy beach with her pail of sand-caked shells and violin case. She stared down at the warped violin case in her arms and began to cry.*

*"Sometimes the broken misfits stay closer to our hearts than a perfect, spotless one would," she'd said.*

*Her mother had disappeared. All that remained of her were her fading footprints in the sand...*

There was a loud pounding on the door.

Daphne jolted awake, her throat clogged with tears she was trying to restrain. Her pillow felt lumpy beneath her head as she tried to gather her bearings. The dream...the beach and her mother and the poor broken starfish... it had seemed so real. And like every dream she had of her mother, she always vanished before Daphne could prevent it.

"Daphne! You're going to be late!" her father warned through the door.

Daphne vaulted out of bed, realizing that she had once again forgotten to set her alarm clock the night before. She pulled on a pair of wrinkled blue jeans lying on the floor along with a clean t-shirt from her closet.

Her dad had already buttered some toast for her. Spreading on some jam and spilling her glass of orange juice in her haste, Daphne quickly ate and mopped up the mess. She rushed back to her room to gather her schoolbooks and stuff them in her back-pack. Daphne felt her heart skip a beat and flutter wildly. She found herself staring into the shadows beneath her bed where the mysterious violin rested. It had been in her dream as well, she remembered. It had washed up at her feet from the ocean.

Daphne couldn't help but pull the violin case out. Her heart was pounding, rushing blood to her ears. Was the sad dream still upon her, or was she trem-bling just because she wondered what she would find inside?

She gasped with what she discovered. The letter she had addressed to Damon Ledger, which she had put directly on top of the violin, was gone. Just like her mother in the terrible dream, the letter had vanished. Daphne searched every part of the case; she even looked inside the violin, but it was useless. Her letter was gone.

A funny sensation crawled over her skin, and a shiver went down her back. She began to close the case when something white caught her eye. Her letter? Daphne pulled the envelope from the hidden pouch with apprehension. She had just searched there. She must have somehow skimmed over it.

But no, it was not the letter she had written. For a moment, everything seemed to melt away as she stared at the envelope penned with dark ink: To Miss Daphne Palmer followed with her address.

Someone must be pulling a prank on her. It had to be Dad. Her father was like that. But the more Daphne tried to use that excuse, the more she realized that it could not be true. Her father knew nothing of the letter—he didn't even know about the violin. The violin case had been hidden under her bed.

It was Damon's handwriting, whoever he was. He had written her name with that beautiful handwriting of his that made hers look like chicken scratching. And her letter to him was missing. What could this mean...?

"Daph! You need to be out the door right now!"

She jumped. She had forgotten all about school. Daphne stood and slung the bag of books onto her back. The letter to her from Damon was still in her hand. She had no time to read it now. It would have to wait.

Gently, Daphne folded it and slipped it into her pocket, marveling over what could be written inside.

Kissing her father good-bye, she dashed out the door, hopped on her bike and rushed to school.

✧

Daphne could hardly concentrate all during her first period of school. She sat silently at her desk, pencil frozen in hand over her open book, and her mind swarming with questions that had no answers. She could feel the thick envelope folded awkwardly in her pocket. Her fingers yearned to rip it open, and yet she dared not touch it, especially there in class, as Mr. Henderson was writing an algebra problem on the board and his monotone voice droned on and on.

Finally, the bell rang and Daphne went through the usual routine getting through the hall to her locker. Shoving her books into the locker, Daphne spun around only to smack into a tall body. Ivan. She should've known.

"Hey Daphne," Ivan said with a small smile. "I was looking for you. I wanted to ask you something…"

No, not here, not now. Why me? Daphne felt her skin chill.

Ivan was tall. His long brown hair was shaggy and tangled, shielding his eyes as if he didn't want people to see him.

"I…I don't have time now," Daphne said faintly, catching sight of the popular Mallory Geris walking by staring at them as if Daphne and Ivan were aliens.

"I have to go," Daphne all but burst away and rushed to the restroom.

She passed several girls gathered around the mirrors and locked herself in an empty stall. Daphne yanked the letter out with such force that she even surprised herself.

Just forget about Ivan. Forget about him. He just wants help with his homework. He can ask someone else to do it. Daphne shivered and stared at the letter.

Several girls were gossiping and laughing, but she scarcely heard them.

Her finger was jutting beneath the sealed envelope and ripping it open. Unfolding the letter, she began to read.

*Friday, April 12, 1912*

*Dear Miss Palmer,*
*You can imagine the shock I received when I found the letter from you resting in my violin case last night.*

*How did you find the letter I wrote yesterday? I pitched it over the side of the ship and watched it disappear underneath the water with my own eyes. And surely the water would have smeared the ink and the paper would have been utterly destroyed.*

*That is why I find this very odd and appalling!*

*How on earth (if you will pardon my brash manners) did*

you get inside my quarters and set your letter in my violin case?

Are you aboard this ship? If that is so, then who are you?

If you would, kindly explain to me why you call the year 2002? It is 1912. And I am not 111 years old. As I mentioned before, I am 18.

You claim that you have my violin. You must be writing in jest because my violin is here with me. You also claim you reside in Atlanta. Do you by any chance mean the United States of America? I have never been to America, although this voyage's destination is New York.

You also seemed oblivious to what the White Star Line is. Well, allow me to enlighten you. It is a big company that is constructing the most luxurious ship liners in the world. And I am more than appreciative to be in their fine service.

As you can detect, I have numerous questions and I do not understand what this is about. Maybe this has originated from my feverish imagination, and my desperate longing for someone to correspond with and befriend. Yet I cannot convince myself that this is not real. I am going to throw this letter over the side of the ship. And if it gets to you, Miss Daphne Palmer, I will begin to consider that I truly may be corresponding with someone from the time of my future.

                                        Respectfully yours,
                                        Damon Ledger

Daphne stared at it in shock. She felt as if his words had slapped her in the face. She tried to gather her wits, but they seemed to be flying every which direction out of her desperate reach. Her palms were cold and clammy as she stuffed his letter back into her pocket. That was when she became aware of how quiet it was. Everyone had left. How long had Daphne been there? Drawing in a deep breath that seemed to release a tremor throughout her entire being, Daphne told herself to get on to class.

One side of her wanted to forget that any of this had happened—to deny it. But then there was the other side, hungry to discover what could happen. She slowly began to understand that she was somehow corresponding with a man in the past. Their connection had broken through time.

It couldn't happen. And yet it had!

If only somehow she could convince Damon Ledger that he was doing the same, only he was tangled in time with the future.

✢

Damon Ledger stood at the rail of his ship's deck. He had just dropped the letter addressed to Daphne Palmer into the water. The wind had made it flutter and flip, and then he saw it. Right when the envelope hit the ocean's foamy waves, it had promptly disappeared—not sunk—just disappeared.

He stared at it with dazed eyes. The possibility of being connected to someone 90 years ahead of him frightened him. Things like this could not happen. He was just an ordinary young man.

Damon pulled away from the rail, the piercing April wind coming off the face of the water sending an icy chill through his body. Was it just the wind making him shiver or the fact that he had just responded to a woman of the future?

Damon wasn't sure. He could hardly think as he walked about the deck cramming his hands into his pockets to shield them from the relentless cold bite of the air. The first leg of the voyage had gone rather smoothly, or so Damon thought. The ship's last boarding stop had been at Queenstown, where Damon was beginning to regret tossing that one foolish letter overboard.

His job and tasks had been simple and almost enjoyable, probably because of the excited atmosphere of the voyage that rubbed off on everyone. Damon was a room steward for a few First Class passengers. For the most part they were agreeable and grateful for his service.

The ship was so monstrous that Damon had already gotten lost and turned around several times. There were so many rooms—and even more people.

Damon nodded politely to a lady and man dressed warmly in furs who passed him as they strolled on the Promenade. Then he turned into the ship's smoking room to get warm for a moment. The room smelled heavily of the sharp, acrid smoke from the gentlemen's cigars. Looking around he observed wealthy, powerful men, some of whom had probably been there since the night before, addicted to their nightly gambling. They had playing cards splayed in their hands. Rambunctious laughter erupted from them when a joke was shared, their elbows rattling their crystal whisky glasses and brandy snifters.

The round clock, which was carved into a mahogany wooden wall piece, chimed half past seven. Damon's momentary diversion was over. He knew he had to get back to work.

*3*

Daphne recklessly biked home. She didn't care that it was pouring rain. She just needed to get home to write a letter to Damon.

With her long hair dripping wet and plastered to her face, she had come to accept the truth of Damon Ledger. Thinking about him all day long at school had forced her to accept his existence. He was living right now, the same month and day, only he was in 1912. How their letters managed to cheat time, traveling back and forth across 90 years, she could not begin to understand. She only knew she wanted to know more of this Damon Ledger.

She peddled into her driveway and got off her bike, throwing it down at the edge of the concrete and cutting across the yard. It was the shortest way to get in the house and she had no time to waste.

Her father, as usual, hadn't gotten home yet, so Daphne unlocked the back door with her own house key. She raced to her room, dropping her backpack along the way, her sneakers squeaked loudly over the hardware floors. She kicked them off once inside her room and sat at her desk, despite her sopping wet clothes that were creating puddles on the floor.

Daphne got Damon's letter out and read it again. She had read it countless times throughout the day. She had almost memorized the unique curve of each of his written words and every crease and fold of the paper, now wrinkled and somewhat smeared by the rain. In a way, Mr. Ledger sounded impertinent, but how could she blame him? He was obviously con-fused.

It felt as if her heart hesitated a moment as she wondered how she would write to him. Setting his letter down, she got a fresh sheet of paper and a pencil.

For a minute she simply sat there, lost in a whirl of words and emotions that she was eager to write to him, to convince him of what was happening to them. Then she was scared and worried that he might not believe her no matter what she wrote.

Sighing, Daphne picked up her pencil and began to write:

*Friday, April 12, 2002*

*Dear Damon Ledger,*
*Believe me, I was just as surprised as you when I opened "our"*

violin case and saw the letter I had placed in there for you gone and the one you had written me in its place.

Thank you for explaining to me what the White Star Line was, but I'm sorry to tell you that it doesn't exist any more (at least not to my knowledge). No one really travels much by ship any more. When we desire to cross the ocean; we usually travel by planes—in the air. I hope it doesn't sound too ridiculous to you, but I myself have flown in a plane across the Atlantic Ocean.

It sounds as if you don't want to believe that we are corresponding through a passage of time. But there's no other explanation.

I wrote that letter to you just for the fun of it at first, and then I stuck it into the violin case without much thought. This morning, however, my letter had vanished and your letter to me was there instead.

I have thought this whole afternoon about it and pondered over your recent letter. I see this as more of a privilege than a curse. Of course, you may think otherwise, but think just for a moment about all that we could learn from each other. You in the past and me in the future. I wish to know all about you and your way of life, but I don't want you to write just because I am urging you to. I beg you only to write again if you feel the same deep fire in your heart and if you do not feel too bewildered.

Sincerely,

Daphne Palmer

Daphne got an envelope and tucked the letter inside. And like the night before, she wrote "To Damon Ledger" on the front and sealed it.

Propping the violin case onto her bed, she opened it and placed the letter on top of the violin. Sighing heavily and her heart suddenly pounding, she shut the case. Daphne waited for a minute, which seemed to last an eternity. Then she opened the case again.

Her letter to Damon Ledger was gone.

✢

Damon was in one of his passenger's empty rooms making the bed with clean, fresh sheets, when there came a tightening inside his chest. He cleared his throat and fluffed the silky pillows, but the strain and tugging inside of him would not let up. He suddenly could scarcely breathe and forced himself to sit in a nearby chair.

He knew exactly what was causing it. Daphne had just sent him a letter. He had felt the exact strange sensation when this Daphne girl had sent him the first note. Damon tried to push aside the curiosity from his mind of what she could have written to him as he stood and went to the porthole and wiped it clean of finger prints.

But the pain became so intense that he was forced to leave the room and hurry to his quarters—trying not to arouse suspicion from the other bedroom stewards walking down the hallways with piles of fresh linens and pillows.

The strain seemed ready to tear his heart in two by the time he made it to his bunk. Damon was more than grateful to be alone, seeing that his three other roommates were gone and their little quarters quiet except for the gentle humming of the ship's engine beneath his feet.

Damon pulled his violin out from beneath his berth. Flipping up the case he saw that there was indeed a letter for him from Daphne resting on top of the violin.

"I thought for sure she wouldn't respond," Damon murmured to himself aloud as if the envelope had ears to hear him. He sat down on his berth and made time to read the letter.

Traveling by air in an airplane seemed very familiar to her. Crossing the Atlantic Ocean onboard a plane sounded as if she did it every other month.

In 1908, Wilbur Wright of America had brought one of his planes on a spectacular tour through France, staying in the air for a flight record of 2 hours and 20 minutes. Damon had been 14, but he remembered the stir among his companions at the academy over the achievement. And not but two years ago, a French design of a sea plane had made a successful flight.

White Star Line no longer remained? It pained

Damon. He chewed on his fingernail as he read, and then again muttered aloud to himself: "so you happen to reside in the year 2002, Miss Palmer. How do you suppose this ever happened?"

He shoved her letter in his knapsack, which he also kept stored beneath his berth, and tore a blank page from his journal. His sister Flossy had given the leather-bound journal to him when she had discovered that he was leaving. It was for him to write all of his seafaring adventures down so she could read them when he returned someday. He didn't have the heart to inform her that he may never be back, not with the way Father was treating him.

Shaking away the painful memories, he got comfortable on his stiff, thin mattress and quickly began to write.

*Friday, April 12, 1912*

*Dear Miss Palmer,*
*You have done a fine job convincing me that you are a woman of the future. Your writing of traveling commonly by air fascinates me. I have never been on a plane, but there have been pictures of Wilbur and Orville Wright's plane in the newspapers. To think I thought the ship I now walk upon was incredible and would never be challenged in the future! It now seems to me as if I must look at all my surroundings*

*with awareness, wondering if they too might survive the long years between us to be useful in your time.*

*Now that I have mentioned it, tell me more of your day. Have you ever been to London? Can you tell me anything of it now? I hope you do not consider this brash, but what kind of clothes do you wear in your time? Is it possible for you to send me a photograph of yourself? If it is too expensive or difficult for you to do, I understand. But I suddenly am curious to know what your appearance is. You know my age, but I have yet to learn yours. And would there be any suitors there to court you, that is if you are not married yet, of course.*

*I must return to my duty, but I await your next letter.*

*Respectfully yours,*
*Damon Ledger*

Damon quickly folded it, unable to find an envelope, and wrote Daphne's name. Then he slipped it into his large side pocket and put his knapsack and violin case away in their place. Striding out to the boat deck, he made sure no one was noticing him. Then he brought the folded letter into his hands and let the wind hurtle it from his grasp and down to the ocean.

✣

Daphne was in the middle of her homework when she felt the unmistakable heart beat inside her. *Damon.* She was just about to put her pencil down and shut her miserable schoolbook and go for the violin case when there came a heavy pounding on the door.

"Daphne Joy, I hope you have a good explanation."

The tone of her father's voice clearly told her that he was in a foul mood.

Daphne jumped to her feet, tripping over her backpack that lay sprawled with books and papers on the floor, and opened the door.

"What's wrong?"

"Don't 'what's wrong' me," her father boomed. "I heard you skipped history class today. And you left your bike right in the driveway. I about ran over it! You also tracked mud all over the den and hallway. I know that's not like you. What's your reason for this behavior?"

Daphne wanted more than anything for the floor to open up and swallow her. She couldn't tell her father about the letters. He wouldn't believe her and would think she had gone daft and that Damon Ledger was no more than her high-strung imaginary friend. That's how her father was. He was realistic. His job as a lawyer made him see every side of the picture with all fantasies omitted. Maybe it was because they had lived in Florida with Mother and everything had seemed so perfect, just like a fantasy, until Mom had been taken...

She hated to lie, especially to her father. Even with all her drama practices and classes, Daphne felt as if she couldn't conceal the truth. And her dad was the one who would see it if she tried.

"I, I wasn't feeling good, Daddy," Daphne groaned. That was actually true. "I sat out of history because I felt like I was going to be sick. I sat in the rest room the entire time."

"Why didn't you call me? Or talk to the school nurse?" Her father demanded. He looked worn and irritated, but there was still that gentle love he felt towards Daphne deep in his tone.

"I don't know!" Daphne cried. Her heart was thundering inside of her, almost making it impossible to breathe. All she could think about was the letter that she knew lay inside the case for her. She must have sounded breathless because Mr. Palmer cocked his head and all annoyance had left his face.

"You do look ill," he said as he put his large hand on her forehead. "You feel warm and...is that sweat?"

"I'm fine, Dad, really. It's just hot in here."

"Should I make a doctor's appointment?" Now he was concerned. Once her father made up his mind to do something, there was almost no way to convince him otherwise. For a fleeting second, Daphne thought she saw the same fearful light in his eyes that had become a part of him when Mother was sick and dying. He was backing away, already heading for the phone.

"Dad, no, I'm fine. How about we wait until tomorrow and see how I feel then?" Daphne called.

Her father paused, and then slowly nodded in consent. "Fine, if that's what you want. I put your bike up in the garage for you, but the mud is still on the floor—"

"I'll clean it up," Daphne offered, the tugging inside subsiding for a moment.

"If you feel like it…"

"I'm fine." She smiled to convince him and then followed him into the kitchen to get some cleaner. She wiped up the red mud she had tracked in and returned to her room, leaning on the door after she had shut it. From the other room she could hear her father talking on the phone with one of his clients.

Finally, she knelt by her bed and brought out the violin.

She read through Damon's letter several times, smiling at some of his comments. She could almost hear his voice, echoing through the tunnel of time to reach her, and feel the wit and charm he didn't know he possessed.

Rummaging through her desk drawer, Daphne found a pile of pictures.

Forgetting her homework, she leafed through the pictures. Most of them were of when she had lived in Florida. Daphne sighed, wondering which one to send him when one of the photos slipped from her grip and landed face down on the floor. She bent over to scoop it up only to pause when she saw that it was a picture of her mom and her, sitting on the golden sand of their favorite spot at the beach.

Her mother was wearing sunglasses and had a baseball cap on, and her arm around Daphne. They were both smiling, probably because her dad was making funny noises when he had taken the picture (like he always used to do). Daphne had a pair of old, patched overalls on, and her hair was free and blowing with the wild frenzy of the wind. It had been a happy time for them. She recalled it with a cold pain forming inside of her. It was the last picture they had taken before her mother was diagnosed with leukemia.

For some reason, Daphne felt compelled to put this picture with her next letter. She sat at her desk, pushing her homework aside, and set the picture down before her. She took her time writing Damon. When she was done and satisfied, she slipped the picture in with the letter over the violin.

Friday, April 12, 2002

Dear Damon Ledger,
I find your questions and comments quite peculiar, but since
you wrote me back, I will reward you with the answers and
try to tell you a little about my time.

Airplanes are a lot of fun to ride on. You can look out your
window and see cars and trees merely as dots and clouds
streaking by. You don't feel like you're flying until you hit
turbulence (little pockets of rough air that make the plane
bounce). You have your own seat and most of the time you
have to keep your seatbelt buckled, although it is not manda-
tory. If you're going on a long flight, the flight attendants
serve you drinks and refreshments and even dinner and
breakfast. There's also a latrine in case you must answer
nature's call or settle your stomach.

I've never been to London so I'm afraid I cannot answer
you there. I have been to Paris, France and Munich, Germany
with my Dad because he travels a lot, and his brother lives in
Europe.

As for clothes, I usually just wear blue jeans and a t-shirt. Weather in Atlanta is usually hot, sticky, and humid. I like wearing flip-flops because you can slip them right on and off, but I do wear tennis shoes when I ride my bike (which is often). Dad wants me to dress more nicely, especially at school, since one time the principal complained that my jeans had a rip in the back pocket, but I'd rather not. But to appease my dad, I wear dresses on Sunday to church.

I'm 16 years old, only two years younger than you (if you forget the 90 years in between), and there are no "suitors" as you call them. And I'm of course NOT married. But I will forgive you for that strange comment, for you didn't know my age, so how could you know?

I've enclosed a picture of myself for you to have. And don't worry, it didn't cost me anything. I've got so many pictures scattered about my room that I need to organize them. The woman with me is my mother. We used to live only minutes away from the beach, so we would go there every day, until she became very sick with cancer.

I remember her one day getting really short of breath and suddenly weak when we were riding bikes at the beach. She convinced me that she was just tired and hadn't been getting enough sleep lately. A few days later she had a high fever, but she refused to let my father take her to the doctor. When it became worse, my dad finally called an ambulance to take her to the hospital. The doctors found her to have acute myeloid leukemia. It's a cancer of the blood cells. She decided *to undergo chemotherapy, which made her terribly sick. I hate to remember my life at that time. And then she got an infection and passed away.*

*My father and I had a hard time getting over what had happened. Our house suddenly seemed dark, empty, and too quiet. Even our favorite restaurant didn't cheer us up because it was Mom's favorite, too. I hated going to the beach because it was a constant reminder that my mother was gone and wasn't coming back. So Dad decided that we would move. That's when we came to Atlanta, and that's why I have no friends. I didn't even have very many friends in Florida. I always had my mom. And if I happened to befriend a girl my age at my old house in Florida, it was usually in the summer when she was spending her family vacation down there, and then she left with the approach of autumn.*

*Wow, I see now that I've babbled a lot more than I thought I would, but I feel as if you will listen, Damon Ledger. Even if you are far away from me.*

*I hate closing a letter in a sad mood, so maybe you can answer some of my own questions.*

*What do you do on your ship? Do you like it? I'm sure it's a wonderful job, so please write me and tell me about it. I'm afraid I've never been on a boat—or ship—so, maybe you could explain to me what it's like.*

*What do you look like? Are you tall? Short? Brown-eyed? Blonde-haired? Do you have a beard? Sorry if I seem too forward. I've been sitting here trying to imagine what you*

*could possibly look like, but no image comes to my mind.*
*Please write back.*

*Sincerely,*
*Daphne Palmer*

In his bunk he read the letter from Daphne. She had sent it to him late in the afternoon, but his duties had restricted him from reading it until now. He had done his chores with her letter tucked unopened snugly within the breast pocket of his uniform. Every time Damon bent over to clean the floor or carpet, he heard the envelope crinkle, and constantly pondered what Daphne had written him.

It was around eleven at night, and he was tired after a full day's work. But reading Daphne's letter put a smile on his lips. He could just about imagine her voice, rippling through the crack of time.

And then he read about her mother and saw the picture, and feelings of his own pain were aroused. There was Daphne, sitting beside her mom on a sandy beach. He hadn't imagined that she was so beautiful. He really hadn't thought much about what she looked like until that afternoon. She appeared so happy there with her mother, Daphne's eyes so blue they glittered like sapphires. They were both smiling so that Damon almost felt their laughter warm his skin.

He held the picture in his hand and stared at it. The picture was so thin that he could bend it. Like paper. And it was full of color. He couldn't believe that Daphne wore men's clothes every day except for Sunday mornings. And the odd and blunt way she worded things!

"There is a latrine in case you must answer nature's call or settle your stomach." No woman of 1912 would utter such a phrase to a man, and at first Damon was shocked. Then he laughed.

"What's that you got there, Ledger?" One of Damon's roommates, a short Scottish man named Billy, asked with his thick brogue, from across the room where he was sitting on his berth buffing his shoes. "Letter from a sweetheart?"

"No, from my sister," Damon lied, not wanting them to prod him into reading it aloud as they usually did when one received a letter from a sweetheart. He made sure that the other boys couldn't see Daphne's picture or see her simple handwriting through the paper. He tore another page out of his journal and wrote by the dim lamp light.

Daphne was just preparing for bed when she felt a stirring, like a gentle breeze on a hillside, gathering leaves within its grasp. She opened the violin case. Her heart skipped a beat when she saw a letter waiting for her.

*Friday night, April 12, 1912*

*Dear Daphne,*
*I hope this letter does not awaken you from sleep, for with me, every time you send a letter, I feel a rushing within my heart and I know something from you has arrived.*

*I appreciate your honesty with me about your mum. Sharing about your mum has made me realize that you have shared a piece of your heart to which I must respond likewise, for my own mum has passed away. I feel the same pain as you—the emptiness and loneliness. If you recall, in my first letter I mentioned that my father has disinherited me because he blames me for my sweet mum's death. And so I must tell you, just as you were fair to tell me, what happened and why I am to blame in my father's eyes.*

*My father has a rather large and beautiful estate in the countryside, and when my mum had tired of the bustle of London, she always desired to retreat to there, where she could walk the lush hills and sit in the beautiful garden there with my sister for company. Roses were always her favorite flowers, and one day I sat with her beneath the canopy beside a lovely bush of red roses, taking tea at our normal time.*

*I remember her commenting on the beautiful weather and temperature of the day, and how brilliant the red roses were that year. She took my hand, for she had always been rather soft and loving to me, more than my father liked. That was when my father arrived in the garden, dressed for a hunt.*

With sharpness in his voice, he told me to prepare to accompany him. He very well knows that I dislike hunting. Nevertheless, that day I wanted to please him and to aspire to what he wanted me to become.

I found a set of hunting apparel on my bed, complete with new polished boots that my father must have purchased for me. Soon my gray steed was saddled and I mounted, following my father and uncle and the pack of hounds. I took my bow and a quiver of arrows, even though my father protested. I thought perhaps he would let me practice my favorite hobby of archery, if I stayed with the hunt long enough to satisfy him.

We rode to woods I had never been through, even though they lay on our property. My uncle sounded the horn and the hounds were wailing and running everywhere at once as they detected a scent.

My father and uncle galloped ahead, paying no heed to me. I had just turned 17 and, although I wanted to please Father, I knew I never would with a hunt, and so I rebelled and halted my horse.

The baying of the hounds and ring of the bugle soon faded in the distance, and nothing but the chirping of birds surrounded me in those woods. I dismounted and prepared my bow and arrows, determined that if Father was going to make me come out there, that I would do something that I liked. In the distance, I saw a huge beehive hanging from a tree. I could not resist as I cocked the arrow to the string and raised the bow. It was a perfect shot. Even the distance was not a struggle for me as my arrow lodged into the hive and the nest fell with a thud. I felt triumphant and then became aware of the terrible, wrathful hissing of angry bees seeking the one who had destroyed their home.

I hastily mounted my horse, now white-eyed with terror, and my horse and I shot out of the woods, down a grassy knoll, and through a creek that wound about our property.

It was not difficult to locate my father and uncle. The hounds were still baying and the bugle sounding. My father acted as if he did not know that I had been gone, but I could tell by the way his jaw clenched when I rejoined them that he did indeed know and was vexed at my absence.

We were on our way back to the barn when one of the servants came galloping to meet us on a horse.

"What's the matter, Shirley?" my father asked, reining in his horse.

Shirley was weeping, something that greatly moved me for I had never seen a grown man cry, and his tears reflected the sunlight.

"Sir, there's been an accident," the servant choked out with misery. "It's your wife, Sir. The lady was taking a walk when a swarm of angry bees overtook her and," a deathly pause and my heart ceased to beat, "attacked and killed her."

I don't quite remember what happened then as I screamed and raced back to the house with my father and uncle. I shall never forget the swollen pale face of my dead mum, and the next day when my father discovered the empty beehive on the ground, with my arrow lodged within it.

He cursed at me and beat me with his fierce anger. I knew the love he had for my mum. He swore that I had known she had been walking nearby and I still shot the beehive down. And so he denounced me of my inheritance, claiming that if I wanted to keep food in my mouth after I became 18, I would have to do it on my own.

And so here I am, thankful for my employment on this ship and for your letters, Daphne. My only desire is that I could really see you. I wish that there was no barrier between us. Time has brought us together, and yet at the same time, it cruelly keeps us apart.

On board the ship, I'm simply a room steward. I have my certain passengers to see to, cleaning up after them, and making sure they are always comfortable. The ship is so gigantic that it's hard to find one's way around. It's very cold on deck but refreshing. There are countless rooms to visit; including a gymnasium and a swimming pool down on one of the lower decks (I still have not seen it yet).

As for what I look like, I have enclosed the only picture I have of myself in this letter for you.

I'm tall, brown-eyed, dark-haired, and I do not have a beard or mustache, for I find them too bothersome. I know the picture is in black and white, and nothing compared to the beautiful colored one you sent to me, but I hope you'll approve of it.

Please write to me again soon. I find that your letters are the only light in my day.

Affectionately,
Damon Ledger

Daphne pulled out the hard board picture. Even if he was absolutely ugly to the eye, she still would have thought him lovely and handsome after the piece of his heart he had just handed to her in that letter.

The picture of his face was clear. It cut off around his chest with a fuzzy line, and despite the lack of color, he was definitely handsome.

He had a firm jaw, probably inherited from his father, and a clean-shaven face. His nose was dramatic, and his eyes so lonely and lovely that it made Daphne want to cry. His hair was dark and had some curl where it brushed against his forehead. His expression was as serious as the grave.

Somehow, Daphne felt as if she had known him all her life. She felt as if she had been sitting with him and his mother beneath the canopy surrounded by the roses, that she had been there the day of the hunt and that she had been standing right beside him when he shot his arrow.

Slightly smiling and brushing her fingers over the face of Damon's picture, Daphne suddenly remembered the words that her mother had spoken in her dream the night before. "Sometimes the broken misfits stay closer to our hearts than a perfect, spotless one would…"

Daphne stared down at Damon's picture once again and she saw a starfish with a broken leg. It'll grow back; it just needs the love and care to make it able to.

Daphne found some paper, grabbed the first writing utensil she could find and wrote:

*Friday night, April 12, 2002*

*My dear Damon,*
*I cannot let your final letter of the night end to me in such a way. I continue to think about you and what you must have felt—and still feel—about everything that has happened to you and about your mother. Know that I feel your pain and desolation as you have felt mine, and that I believe that time has not just let this happen, but has selected us for each other.*
  *I'm thinking of you.*

                              *Yours,*
                              *Daphne*


Daphne didn't have to wait long for a reply after she put it in the violin case. She had remained sitting on the floor, re-reading his poetic but sad letter when he replied to her. They were responding to each other so fast that time hardly seemed to be a barrier anymore.

*Dear Daphne,*
*I know it is dreadfully late and that you must get on to bed, as all my mates here have, but I cannot wait in writing a response to inform you that I think exactly as you do. Could it only have been this morning that I first wrote to you? How*

*does time move so quickly upon us, or can it possibly be we that have driven our companionship to a deeper vein? Well, the lamp is flickering. I will take it as a sign to turn it off. Good night.*

*Damon*

Damon was disappointed in the morning that no letter from Daphne had come. He was busy the entire morning for one of his passengers had a "stifling headache" and another wanted to order three dozen roses to enlighten her room. There seemed to be more cleaning to be done than usual, and Damon was beginning to become annoyed at the constant demands on his attention.

To make things worse, he was at odds with his roommate Billy over a silly matter. Damon hated to be at odds with anybody because it reminded him of the terrible, dark gap now between him and his father. It was the first time that he ever thought of returning home sometime in the future and trying to mend the bitterness that kept his father estranged from him.

He strode up and down the red-carpeted hallways, going in and out of rooms, answering the impatient bells that the passengers were sounding every few minutes. One complained that the breakfast tray Damon had brought to him had been cold, and another passenger wanted to argue about something in the latest news of the ship that Damon had passed out.

It was more than he could bear.

In his pocket was the picture of Daphne that he would ever so often sneak out into his palm to gaze upon. If only she would write him. Then he could go on with the day. He was surprised at how he was coming to depend on her letters.

While Damon was busy dusting one of his passenger's vacant rooms, he paused quickly to pull the picture out of his pocket.

Where was she? Why hadn't she written him? Had he been too forward? Had he told her too much of his past and now she was reconsidering keeping a correspondence going with him?

"You're getting ahead of yourself, Damon," he muttered as he tucked the picture away, pushing back a curl of his hair that kept falling in his face and irritating him. "It's only ten o' clock in the morning. Give her some time. Most Americans appreciate sleep in the mornings."

At first, the idea of corresponding with her had seemed ludicrous and a complete waste of time to Damon. He thought that she was somehow fooling him by pretending to be in the future. But he felt differently now. He knew it was true and he found that he not only wanted but needed her letters.

At noon, Damon was walking by the passenger's dining saloon and looked in. The sounds of the chattering of people and the scraping of cutlery on plates floated about in the air with the background music of a string quartet. He stared over the heads of the people and could see the lead violinist in the corner playing the sweet melody that drifted over all the talking and clattering of dishes. The violin's voice seemed to be the only thing that reached Damon's ears. Daphne plays the violin, he thought. All his thoughts came back to her.

The dining room was wide and full of sunlight. The appealing fragrance of freshly-steamed tea, tart dressings, and roasted meats wafted behind the white-coated waiters who seemed to float from table to table with silver platters or rolling trays. The food smelled wonderful, and this was his scheduled time to eat a mid-day meal. But, because the crew could never eat with the passengers in the dining room, he went below to the crew's dining room. By the time he got there he had decided he wasn't hungry, but he could have a cup of tea. No matter how hard he tried, Damon could not adapt to the American's coffee. It was terribly bitter to him and many of his fellow Englishmen. He poured himself a cup of the hot liquid and sat down at an empty table where he kept running his fingers up and down the table absent-mindedly.

Surely she had gotten his last letter. He had sent it quite late, but surely she would have gotten it by now.

As he sat there feeling completely alone in a room full of crew members, a thought suddenly dawned on him. What if he could no longer reach Daphne? What if the law of time had finally closed the gap in which they had corresponded? The thought saddened him a great deal and he pushed his teacup away.

He got to his feet and slowly walked to his room. He tore a blank page out of his journal, took a pen and sat down on his berth with an empty sigh.

His letter was brief, for time was precious and his mind felt devoid of words at the moment. Then he gently folded it and dropped it over the side of the ship when he went back on deck. The letter disappeared, just like always. So Damon was convinced that he was still in connection with Daphne. But the question now was: why wasn't she responding?

✧

Daphne didn't arrive home until five in the evening that Saturday. She knew Damon had sent her a letter because she could feel the strain all day. She couldn't concentrate at all during drama class or her long violin lesson, and now she really regretted not writing him that morning.

Wearily setting down her play script and storing

her instrument in her closet, Daphne pulled out the old violin case and sat beside it on the floor. She opened it and found two letters from Damon waiting in the violin. No wonder she had felt so exhausted all day; never before had she received two letters at once from him.

She eagerly unfolded the first.

*Saturday, April 13, 1912*

*Dear Daphne,*
*As I sit on my berth I wonder why you haven't written me. Have I said something that offended you? Are you vexed with me? I cannot decide what may be wrong, but all I know is this, Daphne. Please don't stop writing to me.*

*At first, I confess, I thought our letters were foolish and counterfeit. But now, I know that you are the only dear friend I have, even if our letters are the only thing that keeps us together.*

*Please write soon.*

*Always yours,*
*Damon*

✤

*Saturday, April 13, 2002*

*My Dear Damon,*
*Forgive me if I seemed to be gone from you today. Oh how I wished to just stay at home and write to you, but of course, I*

*always have something to do or be at, no matter what day of the week it is. I was gone all day until now at drama practice and then to violin lessons, which took particularly longer than normal because of my upcoming recital, and I needed to practice more with my instructor. And then my father had important errands he couldn't stave off for me to get home sooner.*

*I'm so sorry. I now realize my mistake. I should have written you this morning and explained to you where I would be... but for some reason I thought you, well, wouldn't really want my letters so much. I thought you'd be too busy on the ship to even notice that I hadn't written. I enjoy yours so much, but my own letters seem sloppy compared to your poetic ones.*

*Never, never, have I been mad, or vexed, at you, my dear Damon!*

*I still have another letter of yours to read, so I'm going to send this one on to you so you will know I'm still here, and then I'll write you back.*

*Your friend,*
*Daphne*

She put her letter in the violin case and took up his second letter to her. This one had an envelope and the letter seemed to be some type of stationery with bold lettering at the top. But before she could so much as glance over it, her dad was standing at her door announcing that dinner was getting cold on the table.

She reluctantly set the folded letter down and followed her dad into the kitchen.

When she finally returned to her room Daphne grasped the letter that she sensed was important, the letter that she had to leave unread for dinner. She had been thinking about it all through dinner, wondering why she felt drawn to it and so compelled to read its contents. The first thing her eyes saw made everything crash in on her. It was the bold stationery logo at the top of the page.

ON BOARD THE RMS TITANIC
*Saturday, April 13, 1912*

*My dear Daphne,*
*I thought you might like a real letter with some of the ship's stationery. Before I was just tearing out pages from my journal, but I was passing by the reading and writing room and saw a stack of this stationery. I immediately thought of you.*

*I'm sitting on the ship's deck as I write.*

*The sun is bright and strong, but it is still very cold. I have to wear my heavy coat or else I get extremely chilled. Over the deck there is nothing but a flat "land" of blue ocean. It is quite a sight. I find that I like to sit and stare at the forever stretch of ocean that glistens with the sun's reflection. Once I spotted dolphins playing around beside the ship, but that was near Queenstown, Ireland. The sunsets and sunrises are breath-taking. The sun is like a blood-red ball that casts its color upon the face of the water. The only thing I wish for is that you were here beside me.*

*I know these letters are getting to you because every time I drop them over the side into the ocean, they vanish.*

*I figure you are incapable of writing me now, so I will try to wait patiently, although it is hard for someone like me.*

*Know that I think of you and look at your picture more oft than I should. It is the only thing that keeps me from falling into utter despair.*

*Please write me.*

> *Always yours,*
> *Damon*

Tears were burning Daphne's eyes as she drew in a ragged breath. Why hadn't he told her what ship he was on? Or why hadn't she thought to ask? He had always addressed it as "my ship" and "the ship," but never had he written the name. Why? Was that another one of time's quirks?

Daphne felt as if the walls around her were closing in. She wanted to rip the letter to shreds until it no longer existed, and yet she held it next to her beating heart. What was she supposed to do? What could she do? Even if she told Damon the Titanic's horrifying fate, would he believe her? Well, he should believe her! She was 90 years smarter than him! Daphne knew that, whatever she told him, Damon would believe.

"I'll tell him," Daphne whispered, springing to her feet. But something heavy was on her shoulders. It screamed in her ears until it terrified her, and Daphne sat back down. She knew what the weight was: it was the past. It was history. It was time. It was yelling at her, putting its weight and burden on her, ordering her to not change the course of what was to come. *Those who must die must die, and those who must live must learn.* Who had said that? she wondered.

"No," Daphne argued out loud with the thought: "But what of Damon? I have to warn him! I don't care what the past says!"

She grabbed some paper and a pencil, but she didn't know what to write. She yearned to do what was right, but she wanted to save and protect Damon.

For somewhere in the middle of an icy-cold Atlantic Ocean, Damon was aboard the ill-fated RMS TITANIC.

*6*

*Saturday, April 13, 1912*

*My Dear Daphne,*
*I couldn't help but be consumed by worry over you. Then I*
*actually began to believe that you had tired of me and that I*
*would never hear from you again! Now I understand that*
*you could not write to me, and you can be convinced that I*
*find delight in your letters far more than you will know.*

*I must go now; I cannot tarry any longer. But please*
*understand, Lady Daphne, your letters mean so much to me.*
*Why, I am simply a misfit estranged from his family because*
*of his own folly, and yet you write to me of the future and of*
*yourself. Here I will smile goodbye and write back soon—*
*very soon.*

> *Always yours,*
> *Damon*

He was so quick to respond it cast a feeling of guilt
over her. But she could hardly take joy in his last

letter as she read it, even when he seemed to be writing more of his feelings for her. He was on the TITANTIC, which was the only thing that took root in her mind as she sat numb beside the violin case. Daphne faced the worst problem she could have ever imagined. The only thing she knew about the TITANIC was that it struck an iceberg in the middle of the Atlantic on her maiden voyage and sank. And that hundreds of people froze to death in the icy water because there were not enough lifeboats and no ship came to their aid until later.

The horrible thing was that Daphne knew nothing about what day the disaster actually happened, which would be helpful in a situation such as this. All she knew was that it had been at night. Glancing out her window, she saw that the sun had set and shades of twilight had arrived.

No! What if the ship sinks tonight? What of Damon? I have to do something!

Daphne, gripping the pencil tightly in her hand, began to write as fast as she could:

*Saturday, April 13, 2002*

*Damon! You must write me now! Oh gosh! Whenever you get this! Write me! Why didn't you tell me your ship was THE*

*TITANIC?! And it's all my fault, all my fault! Oh Damon, please say you're there.*

*Yours,*
*Daphne*

She didn't even bother to fold it. She tossed it into the violin case and waited.

She sat against the wall with her knees pulled up to her chin. Her heart was still pounding inside her like a hammer. She stared at the violin case with wild eyes, slightly rocking back and forth. Suddenly, the tugging that was so familiar erupted in her chest.

Daphne lunged for the violin case and yanked it open.

*Saturday, April 13, 1912*

*Daphne? Are you alright? Your letter came during dinner, but I gladly left knowing you had written to me. My peers believe I am now a strange man with all my comings and goings to my quarters and then to the boat deck with my letters to you discreetly hidden within my pockets. Let them speculate all they wish. But it sounds like something is distressing you. What is wrong?*

*What do you mean about the ship? Of course it is the TITANIC. I should have told you before. I thought that you would have never heard of it after I read what you said about airplanes and the White Star Line. I supposed the*

*TITANIC would be completely forgotten, even if she was the most luxurious and grandest ocean liner ever built in my time. You sound like something is wrong though. Tell me right after you receive this letter.*

> *Yours always,*
> *Damon*

Daphne tossed the letter down, now more frustrated than ever. She ripped out another sheet of paper from her spiral notebook and lifted her pencil to write, but like before, she paused as if a wall was in front of her. What would she tell him? First, she needed to know exactly when the ship went down.

But what if the ship struck the berg tonight? What if the TITANIC was hastening to its destruction with speed that Daphne and Damon could possibly slow or avoid? Would she be able to feel it if Damon perished before he could write her an explanation? Would she be able to feel the water pour into the gap of time, gradually rising to shut them off from each other forever, just as the water was soon to flood the ship's interior? As long as the ship lived and stayed above the surface, Daphne knew that Damon would be able to reach her.

"It's the ship," Daphne said softly, suddenly feeling a new revelation form within her mind. "It's not just time that has connected us, but the TITANIC. Even if he lives through the disaster, will I still be able to

write to him? The ship will be gone, and so will our
bond. I cannot make him panic," Daphne spoke to
herself, her voice hoarse and hardly above a whisper—yet it sounded so loud in her ears.

*My dear Damon,*
*I don't wish to alarm you. I'm sorry. You just surprised me*
*with the knowledge of your ship. The TITANIC has been*
*remembered throughout the years. No one has forgotten her*
*or her first voyage. She has found her way into storybooks of*
*memorable ship liners. So don't be alarmed. I'm beginning to*
*believe that it's not only time that has brought us in contact*
*with one another, but the ship as well. Now I just wish that I*
*could be with you on the TITANIC and be with you when the*
*end of the voyage arrives. You are my only friend.*

> *Yours forever,*
> *Daphne*

✛

*My dearest Daphne,*
*I know what you were trying to describe to me about time*
*pulling us. Sometimes I think it will simply rip me away*
*from here and drag me into your time by your side. But I*
*would welcome you here with me on the TITANIC just as*
*much.*

*I never pondered that the ship might possibly be our link*
*with one another. Where did you come up with that notion?*
*It is interesting, but don't you think that our letters will*

continue on, even when my short duration on the TITANIC is finished?

I know you are probably tired from your long exhausting day, so I will let you go. Expect a letter from me in the morning.

Yours always,
Damon

✦✦✦✦

The waves were crashing on the sand, washing white foam and broken chips of shells up to the beach. Daphne found herself walking along the shore barefoot again, except she was alone. Her mother was not beside her as usual.

She had her pail in her hand, swinging it with each stride, and she felt the cold bite of the wind as it traversed over the face of the choppy water.

There was a shell at her feet, partly buried in the sand, and Daphne bent to take it when she heard the faint calling of her name.

She stood and squinted up the shoreline to see someone approaching her. The person was still too far away for her to discern the face, but Daphne could tell from the rugged outline against the washed gray sky that it was a man. Daphne felt a stab of recognition as she instantly realized the man was Damon. She caught her breath with joy and excitement.

Something powerful seemed to keep Daphne standing in her place, as if the cost was too heavy to bear if she dared to even take a step forward. So she waited, feeling as if years of time were elapsing between her and Damon as he came to greet her.

Finally, Damon was standing before Daphne. He was very tall and his brown eyes seemed to glitter with the knowledge of something Daphne could not grasp.

"Look Daphne," he said suddenly, pointing to an object being washed up to where they were standing on the packed sand. He bent over and handed a great starfish to Daphne, and she ran the tips of her fingers over the rough surface.

"I thought it was broken," Daphne whispered, feeling as if her voice was growing fainter and harder to push from her constricting throat.

"No, not any more," Damon whispered. His voice was so deep and clear that it seemed to pierce the very depths of the ocean.

He was smiling down at her and his face was radiant as he began to fade away.

"Don't go!" Daphne lunged forward to grasp his arm, but her voice lodged in her throat, lost only to herself. "Don't leave me, Damon!" She tried to cry once again but it was painful to even whisper. She was frustrated and terribly frightened, the familiar feeling of being left alone on the cold beach creeping over her skin and making her tremble.

Damon gripped her hand firmly but gently in response and looked down into her eyes, the contact of his fingers sending a ripple of something like electricity up Daphne's arm. But he was moving away, gradually, going somewhere Daphne could not follow.

*Someone was coming toward Damon, coming to lead him away, Daphne knew it. The woman was dressed in white, her dress and hair streaming in the wind. As the woman came closer Daphne could feel the warmth that radiated off her soul, becoming a balm to her wounds. It was her mother.*

*She smiled at Daphne, who suddenly felt the cold foaming water rush about her ankles, making her sway and lose her tight grip on Damon. His hand was beginning to melt away from Daphne's grasp. She could not hold onto him any more than she could the wind. He was sand slipping through her fingers. She knew that she had to let him go.*

*So she did.*

*She raised her fingers and dropped her arm slowly to her side. Damon began to fade away with Daphne's mother in the fog that swirled about them like a damp cloak. They had disappeared. Only Damon's fading footprints remained in the sand.*

*Daphne remembered that there was still something in her hand: the starfish. She stared down at it. It was no longer broken.*

✦✦✦✦

Morning light flooded in through Daphne's window.

Her dad was already awake, watching the morning news with a cup of coffee in his hand. He looked up when she trudged into the kitchen.

"You're up early," he said thoughtfully.

"Dad," Daphne said as she cleared the morning

grogginess from her throat and tried to casually lean on the counter, "do you by any chance happen to know anything about the TITANIC?"

Mr. Palmer got up from his chair and walked to the stove where he started dumping clumps of pancake batter onto a hot skillet. "The TITANIC? That was the ship that struck that iceberg, wasn't it?" Daphne saw that he wouldn't be of much help. "Do you have a school report coming up or something?"

"Yeah," was all Daphne could say as she set two places at the table. Sunday mornings were pancake and coffee mornings. It had always been a tradition in their family, started by Mom one day when she wanted to have a special breakfast for Sundays.

"Sorry Tiger," her father said, calling her by her affectionate nickname. "You probably know more about it than me. But maybe if you went next door to Mrs. Smith's you could get the information you need. She seems to collect a lot of antiques."

After enough pancakes were cooked for the two of them, and Daphne had poured herself a cup of coffee, they sat at the table.

Daphne stared out the window, seeing the softness of the sunlight and the blueness of the sky framed with clouds. Damon was still alive. The TITANIC must still be whole and complete or else Daphne would know. Her heart was still connected with his. As long as TITANIC lasted, their connection endured. The clear memory of the dream kept nagging at her, appearing in her mind, and making her skin tingle with the dread she knew was going to arrive soon.

Mr. Palmer unfolded the morning paper that was stacked near him on the table. That was another thing the two of them enjoyed doing on Sunday mornings; going through the newspaper. They spent some time in the paper, pointing out different articles or comics that struck them and reading them aloud to one another.

"Well, we need to leave for church in an hour," Mr. Palmer said as he finished the last section of the newspaper, refolded it and got to his feet. "And I thought it might be nice to go out to lunch some- where special, since I've had to work so much lately. What do you say?"

Daphne just smiled. For the first time since her mother's passing, things were beginning to feel differ- ent—but good again—at home.

✢

Daphne was just clearing the table when she felt a letter from Damon arrive. Perfect timing, she thought as she brushed her hands on a rag. Finally, she and Damon were getting the idea of when to contact each other without creating too much stress.

Daphne hurried to her room, remembering

Damon's predicament (of which he still had no knowledge). Her dream plagued her, as touching his hand, hearing his voice, and his drifting away had seemed so real.

*Sunday, April 14, 1912*

*My dear Daphne,*
*The water is so calm today that even the officers on board are commenting about it. As I was standing by the rail early this morning, I overheard one of the officers by the name of Lightoller say that he has never seen the ocean so serene. The temperatures are very frigid at night. There's even been talk of icebergs circulating, but I know that TITANIC is in good hands.*

*I don't expect a letter from you this morning as I under-stand that you are going to church, but please write me in the afternoon.*

> *Yours Always,*
> *Damon*

Daphne shut her eyes and took a deep breath as his words settled into her mind. She was trying not to remember anything of her nightmare.

The water was calm.

Talk of icebergs.

Frigid temperatures at night.

Officers somewhat concerned.

It meant the TITANIC was going to strike the berg tonight.

Tonight!

Daphne's heart fell and she reprimanded herself for not feeling more prepared. She knew that this was going to come. She had to do something or else she would never forgive herself. Did she even dare wonder what might happen if she told Damon what to expect?

With a heavy and troubled spirit, Daphne headed to church with her father. All the while her mind was restlessly trying to think of a way to stop the inevitable.

✣

Once at home after lunch, Daphne walked over to Mrs. Smith's and knocked on the door. Mrs. Smith looked excited to see Daphne, as if she had been expecting her all day. She quickly invited Daphne inside for some fresh iced pound cake.

Daphne sat at the table, her mind dazed yet constantly searching for a solution.

Mrs. Smith handed her guest a slice of cake and then served her some lemonade.

"Tell me, Daphne, what's this visit about?" the old lady sat across from her with a strange gleam in her eyes.

"Well, Mrs. Smith," Daphne didn't know how

much she should say. "I have a report due tomorrow that I totally forgot about, and I need some books to do research."

"What kind of books, dear?"

"Any books or information about the TITANIC. I thought I'd try and see if you had anything."

"You wouldn't be trying to mess with the past, would you, Daphne?"

Daphne couldn't help but drop her fork and stare at Mrs. Smith.

Mrs. Smith gave a little chuckle. "I won't ask for any details, and yes, I do have plenty of information about the TITANIC. More than you'd find in any old book. It's all upstairs in the attic. You're welcome to take anything you see up there because I certainly have no use for it. It's been sitting up there for some time now."

Daphne followed Mrs. Smith up the wooden, narrow flight of stairs to the attic.

Did Mrs. Smith know? Daphne could hardly contain her curiosity as she entered the attic.

"Here are all of my husband's things. He was quite fascinated with the TITANIC himself and stashed quite a bit of it away in that chest over there," Mrs. Smith said as she indicated a large, heavy wooden chest that sat against the wall.

Daphne knelt by it, her fingers trembling as she pushed up the cover.

"I meant to tell you that old violin I gave you was recovered from the disaster sight just two days after the TITANIC sunk. That's why it's so weather-beaten. It must have been floating about the ocean for a while before someone rescued it."

Daphne looked up at Mrs. Smith. Daphne had known it had been so; she had just been waiting for someone else to tell her.

Inside the chest it smelled like old papers and books, and a puff of dust rose up when Daphne moved some of the papers around inside.

Her hands felt a newspaper, and carefully, Daphne pulled it out.

"That's the newspaper that came out that day everyone discovered TITANIC had sunk," Mrs. Smith explained.

Daphne stared at it, amazed that the paper was still in such good shape.

TITANIC DISASTER! GREAT LOSS OF LIFE! The headlines read.

Setting it gently aside, Daphne reached in farther. Old posters of TITANIC, a map of TITANIC'S interior, Walter Lord's book *A Night to Remember* about the TITANIC, a fork and teacup recovered from the TITANIC wreckage… Daphne was amazed at everything she found.

"I don't understand," she said and smiled at Mrs. Smith, "how did your husband get all of this?"

Mrs. Smith gently smiled back and reached into the chest to retrieve something Daphne hadn't noticed yet.

It was a picture from many years ago. Daphne took it when Mrs. Smith handed it to her.

She was staring at the two faces in the photograph, one of an older man with a frosty, cropped white beard and wearing an impeccable uniform. The other face was of a young boy standing proudly beside him.

"Who are they?" Daphne let her voice trail away.

"That's Captain Edward Smith of the TITANIC with my husband," Mrs. Smith replied.

Daphne gasped. "The captain of the TITANIC?"

"Oh yes."

"And that little boy is your husband?"

"Mmhmm," Mrs. Smith seemed to be reflecting on happy memories.

"But how? How did your husband meet the captain?"

"He didn't meet the captain. The captain was my husband's uncle."

Daphne was dumbfounded. The pieces of the puzzle were falling in place now.

"So Captain Smith of the TITANIC was your husband's uncle?"

"That's right. Oh, how my James loved his uncle! I think he practically worshipped him. That picture was taken of them right before the captain set off on the

TITANIC. My James wanted to go along so badly, for it was Captain Smith's last voyage before he retired. James almost got to go, but the plans never worked out."

"When news came of the TITANIC'S sinking and that the captain had gone down with the ship, it crushed James. For as long as he could remember, he had always wanted to be a captain, just like his Uncle Edward. James' father went aboard on one of the cable ships to help recover the bodies and floating relics two days after the sinking, hoping to find the captain's body. It was then that he found the violin, and the fork and teacup. The fork had been stuck into one of the life preservers, and the teacup had been inside one of the floating crates. He gave them to James, wishing to cheer James' spirits. And my husband kept them until the day he died, never forgetting his brave Uncle Edward whom he so admired."

Daphne looked again at the photo and could feel tears burning her eyes.

"After the disaster," Mrs. Smith went on after clearing her throat, "the press was trying to locate as many pictures of the captain as they could. James could've let them use that picture, but he didn't. He was only a young boy of seven at the time and yet he had so much wisdom. From then onward, he collected as many things about the TITANIC as he could. And here they are now, all in his favorite chest."

"I wish I could've met your husband, Mrs. Smith," Daphne said, a lump welling in her throat.

"I know he would've loved you. Anybody who faithfully remembered the TITANIC he loved and would open his heart to. And I know he would've wanted you to have his old belongings here. So take as many as you want, Daphne. For soon I'll be gone and I'd rather have these precious things of my husband's in gentle hands such as yours." Mrs. Smith put her hand on Daphne's shoulder and began to walk back to the stairs.

"You know, you carry his name," Daphne said and Mrs. Smith looked back upon her. "You bear the captain's name. I don't know why I never realized it."

Mrs. Smith just smiled. "Some things are better off to let others discover."

And then the old woman was gone, the stairs creaking beneath her feet as she descended.

Daphne turned back to the chest, staring at the picture of the captain and his little nephew. She put it on top of the newspaper and continued to fish through the contents, careful not to harm anything.

She pulled out a small flag, and gave a small cry of recognition and surprise when she saw that the old hand-held flag had WHITE STAR LINE printed on its white stained fabric.

It reminded her of Damon and how their time was running out.

Fear pulsed through her as Daphne searched for the one thing she really needed. Her fingers ran across a bristly pile of paper. Lifting them out, Daphne realized that the stack of stained papers she was holding had the names of everyone who had been on board the TITANIC. She held her breath. The names in italic printing were the ones who had survived.

I cannot look now! I cannot! Daphne repeated to herself. What would she do if she saw Damon's name not italicized? She might do something irrational.

She put the stack away where it would not tempt her and finally came to the papers she needed. It told the timeline of the TITANIC'S short voyage ever since the ship had set out from Southampton, England.

Daphne scanned the pages until she reached the one she needed—Sunday, April 14, 1912:

9:00 AM: the TITANIC receives an ice warning from the CARONIA.

11:40 AM: Another ice warning comes from the NOORDAM.

1:42 PM: Yet another ice warning is sent by the BALTIC.

1:45 PM: Still another ice warning arrives from the AMERIKA.

7:30 PM: Three iceberg warnings are sent by the CALIFORNIAN.

9:20 PM: Captain Smith goes to bed, ordering Second Officer Lightoller to wake him if there are any problems.

9:40 PM:   Another ice warning comes in, this time from the MESABA.

10:00 PM:  First Officer Murdoch relieves Second Officer Lightoller on the bridge.

10:55 PM:  The CALIFORNIAN, only a few miles away, tries to send another ice warning but the overworked TITANIC telegraph operator tells them to "Shut up!"

11:30 PM:  The telegraph operator on the CALIFORNIAN signs off for the night.

11:40 PM:  TITANIC lookouts Fleet and Lee spot a large iceberg in the calm ocean and call down to the bridge. Officer Moody tells them "Thank you." Officer Murdoch, who is currently in charge, is unable to steer out of the way, and the starboard side of the ship is torn open in the resulting crash.

Daphne glanced down at her wrist watch. It was now 3:50 in the afternoon. The TITANIC had around eight hours until she crashed. "11:40 PM, Sunday night" … Eight hours…

Daphne went on with the timeline in her hands until she came to Monday, April 15, 1912: 2:20 AM: The TITANIC sinks. Approximately 1500 people—passengers and crew—die in the disaster.

Quickly Daphne put everything back into the chest. The only thing she walked out of the attic with was the time frame she had just been reading.

She found Mrs. Smith sitting in her favorite chair in the living room with her calico cat curled up in her lap. There was a rose in her hand.

"Is that all you're going to take, my dear?" Mrs. Smith got to her feet, her cat sliding to the floor.

"Yes, this is all I need. Thank you. I don't know what I would've done…" Daphne halted, wondering if she was saying too much. And besides, with each word she spoke her voice got thicker with emotion. "I… I'll bring this back tomorrow."

"Keep it. I want you to keep it," Mrs. Smith said with such determination that Daphne couldn't refuse her.

"Alright. And thank you again, for everything," Daphne said as Mrs. Smith opened the door.

"Before you go, Daphne, there's just one thing more I want to tell you," Mrs. Smith said.

Daphne waited with eager ears.

"One way we can learn things is to look back upon history and remember the events that have already happened—the good ones and the bad ones. The only other way we learn is when we forget history and it is repeated with more vengeance. Things from the past have already happened, and even if we get a chance to taste them strongly, we cannot interfere. The past must go on as it was. History must not be altered, no matter what the cost."

Daphne stared at the woman, who was practically a

foot shorter than her but held a treasure chest of knowledge and wisdom. She quietly gave Daphne the rose she held in her wrinkled hand. It was in full bloom and rich in color. Daphne knew the rose was from Mrs. Smith's garden.

A silent tear slipped discreetly from Daphne's eye and formed a round crystal on one of the rose petals.

"I will remember the past, and I will not try to change it," Daphne looked up and said softly. No matter what the cost, no matter what the cost...

7

Sunday Night, April 14, 2002

My Dear Damon,
I'm sorry I didn't find a way to write you sooner, but now I
can. I know you are probably busy (like you always are with
your passengers) but I want to take the time to tell you that
if I could've chosen to write you or not, I wouldn't have
hesitated in that I would. Your letters mean so much to me,
more than you can ever figure in a lifetime. Even if all of
this has to end in pain, I would never take back my friend-
ship with you.

   I don't know if you feel it or not, but I feel our time is
coming to an end. We have broken through time's barriers,
but can the rip possibly continue? Time is like a huge wave,
and I see it coming. It will either engulf you or me, and then
we shall never be able to write each other again. Write me
while you still can, before the big wave separates us.

                                        Forever yours,
                                        Daphne

*Sunday Night, April 14, 1912*

*My Daphne,*
*I feel the wave coming as well. I almost feel like once I lose*
*you, I won't be able to write again. But I do not understand*
*what you mean by one of us being carried away. Are you*
*trying to inform me that you are moving away from me, or*
*that I am moving away from you? I have a slight inkling*
*that you know something—something crucial that you are*
*withholding from me. Of course you know about TITANIC,*
*for you say no one of your time has forgotten her or her*
*maiden voyage. Does something terrible happen? I demand*
*you to tell me, Daphne. Don't you think I deserve to know?*

> *Always yours,*
> *Damon*

✤

*11:15 PM*

*My Dear Damon,*
*Just this day I have promised I would not interfere or change*
*the past, for I know it would alter history if I did. It's why I*
*went to my neighbor, Mrs. Smith's. If I hadn't gone to her*
*house, I think I would've tried to prevent what is coming.*
*Now I see that she is right. Even out of my love for you,*
*Damon, I cannot betray time or TITANIC'S fate when it has*
*granted us this chance.*
*I will remember the past, and I will not change it.*

> *Yours forever,*
> *Daphne*

*11:23 PM*

*My Daphne,*
*I noticed that you have now written the time in place of the*
*date, a sign to me that our time is short and yet precious. If*
*you feel that you should conceal the future from me, then I*
*cannot fight you. I do not want to be angry or at odds with*
*you when the time comes for us to separate, although I*
*strongly desire to know the trouble I sense is going to occur.*
*If you will please grant me the knowledge if the TITANIC*
*will be lost, I would be more than thankful.*

*Always yours,*
*Damon*

✤

*11:30 PM*

*My Dear Damon,*
*The time is nearing. Your question breaks my heart. Listen to*
*my words and hurry and do as I tell you. This is my last*
*letter to you. I know if I continue to write you past this*
*moment, I will utterly break my promise. But I want you to*
*write me for as long as you possibly can, and I want you to*
*know that I am here listening to you.*

*Your father loves you, Damon. Please do all you can to*
*mend the gap between you and him. You are his only son, his*
*heritage. I know you will make him proud.*

*Now, after you receive this last letter of mine, take some*
*paper and a pen and rush up to the starboard side of the*
*deck, near the ship's bow.*

*There stand and you shall see TITANIC'S fate.*
*I love you.*

> *Yours Forever,*
> *Daphne*

⁘

## 11:47 PM

*My Dear Daphne,*
*The thought of you keeps me as I stand here on the deck as*
*you instructed me to do. My hands feel frozen as I sit on the*
*deck chair to write to you. And you can see how my hand is*
*trembling.*

*I stood here, like you said, and felt the bitter coldness of*
*the night sting my face. The water was like black glass, and*
*the stars glittered in the sky like silver dust.*

*I wanted to leave, thinking you had led me wrong when I*
*heard a bell ring three times fast from the crow's nest where*
*the lookouts perch and scan the ocean for ice.*

*And then I saw it. A huge, giant figure darker than the*
*night around us loomed from what seems out of nowhere.*
*And it was directly in the path of the TITANIC.*

*I can't explain the shock and disbelief that coursed*
*through me.*

*The air was so sharp that tears were falling fresh from my*
*eyes and freezing on my cheeks. I could not move as I was so*
*filled with horror as, suddenly, the ship made an attempt to*
*veer.*

*At first I thought she was going to clear it, but the iceberg*
*came right up to the ship's starboard side—where you told*

me to go——and I felt a horrid vibrating beneath my feet and heard a dastardly scraping noise.

Chunks of ice began to rain down upon the deck and I slipped trying to avoid getting hit.

Now I sit here, as the ship has ceased propelling forward and pieces of ice are scattered about the deck. Some of the passengers have made a game out of it and are playing football.

But I do not join them.

I cannot laugh nor can I cry.

I feel like I cannot do anything but think about your warnings and words you once wrote me.

Dear Daphne, I have an awful feeling in my heart. I suppose you know more, but since you have vowed not to write me again, I will leave it at peace.

The rose you enclosed in my envelope pleases and calms me at this moment. It is only slightly crushed, but still full in bloom with its deep scarlet petals. It comforts me and brings back happy memories of my mum. Some of the petals have fallen and lay on the deck's floor amongst the shards of ice.

I will try to write more later.

Always yours,
Damon

✤

Early Monday morning, April 15, 1912
12:38 AM

My Dear Daphne,
It has almost been an hour since I last wrote you.

Things aboard are not well at all.

Everyone has been ordered to stand out on boat deck with their life preservers fastened on. It is so cold that I cannot cease my shivering.

The musicians are playing lively music that is somewhat comforting.

Nobody around me seems to be alarmed.

Some officers nearby are trying to load a lifeboat with women and children, but no women seem to want to get in.

I recognized one of the women asked to step into the lifeboat because she was one of my passengers. She simply sneered at the officer and stalked away.

Daphne, they say this is a boat drill, but I believe it naught. For I know the ship struck the iceberg and that now she is starting to list towards the bow. I don't think anybody has yet noticed it. Or maybe they have and they refuse to acknowledge it.

I am going to stop writing and see if I can help load the women into the boats.

                                        Always your,
                                        Damon

                            ⚜

1:22 AM

My Dear Daphne,
The TITANIC is sinking.

Everybody knows it now.

The deck has listed more than when I previously wrote

*you and the dark, icy water seems to be getting closer and closer.*

*Women are now stepping gladly into the boats with their children, except for a few who are stubborn and desire to remain on the ship with their men.*

*Only I find this odd. None of the men are allowed to get into the boats. And it seems as if we are running short on lifeboats!*

*I'm assisting an officer by the name of Murdoch to load the boats on the port side. He appears to be upholding his position quite well and calm, although his face does look a bit taunt and pale.*

*He has a revolver in case we need it.*

*I'll try to write you again before the waters take the ship——and my connection to you.*

Always yours,
Damon

✤

*2:05 AM*

*My Daphne,*
*Almost all of the lifeboats have departed. The deck is so steep I can scarcely walk to the side to throw my letters to you into the sea.*

*Officer Murdoch has released me from my services and told me to try and save my own life.*

*I sit on the deck with my violin case just in the chance*

*that you might try to write me again. I've tucked your rose into the breast pocket of my coat and I can smell its sweet promise.*

*I think of your last letter, and what you told me of my father. I weep when I think of him. If only I could see his face again. I realize you speak the truth of my father, so I have taken the liberty to write him a letter. I do not believe I will survive, so I asked a kind lady to take it with her on one of the lifeboats. She promised she would post it in the mail for me.*

*My hand and heart are so frozen I don't believe I can write for much longer. It is taking me quite some time just to write these few words. I can only imagine how cold the awaiting water is.*

*The musicians continue to play. The music is so comforting...*

*Men are wandering around the deck, some with stoic expressions on their faces. Others are as frightened as children lost in the dark and have tried to sneak into the few remaining lifeboats being lowered with the women. Of course the officers will have none of this, Daph, and they yank those men right back out and plop them on the deck with a definite thud.*

*I know the TITANIC will not last much longer.*

*No other ship has come to assist us.*

*There are not enough lifeboats.*

*The distress rockets the officers were flaring in the sky have come to an end.*

*Now I understand why you didn't write me again, Daph.*
*I understand.*
*The captain has just released the crew from their duties.*
*It is now every man for himself.*
*Everyone is screaming and pushing.*
*But I sit here on my crooked bench.*
*I'm not going to move.*
*All around me the passengers are jumping over the side of the ship in their distress and hitting the water with a ghastly sound.*
*I hear the water starting to roar up the deck, tilting the ship even more so.*
*All sorts of objects and bodies are slipping down the deck.*
*Daphne, I cannot write any longer.*
*The water is at my feet.*
*My violin case has fallen over the side of the ship.*
*I believe I will simply let the water take this final letter from my hand and deliver its last to you.*
*I know my time has come.*

> *I Love You,*
> *Damon*

# Epilogue

*Tuesday, April 16, 1912*

My Damon is gone. My white star has fallen.
He lies with the TITANIC on the ocean floor, and
with him is a part of me. I still cannot believe he is
gone. I don't want to believe it. I feel like it's my fault
and that I can never forgive myself for losing him.

But then Mrs. Smith's words come back to mind.
She knew about Damon and me. I have to keep telling
myself that what I did was for the best—even though
it hurt.

Why time chose Damon and me with the TITANIC
as our link, I don't know. Perhaps someday I'll learn.

I now realize that some people come into your life
for a purpose. I remember that I used to think only of
myself and my misery of being alone. I am not the
only starfish in the sea with a broken arm. There are
others, in my life, just like Damon, just like me. It is
time for me to look up and see them.

How is it that one can come to know another so
well when they haven't ever actually heard each
other's voices, or seen their faces closely, or touched
their hands?

My father says life is like a vapor. It's here only for a

short while before the sun rises and melts it away. Then it's gone.

I have lost Damon now, but I will gain him again. Until then, he is music in my heart.

> To whoever may be reading,
> *Daphne Palmer*

✠✠✠✠

*Saturday, April 20, 1912*

"Sir, a letter has arrived."

"Set it on the table, Shirley," he ordered.

The servant bowed and quietly set the envelope on the small table beside his master's chair.

Mr. Ledger sat staring through the sunlit window panes into what once had been the rose garden. It was a while before he set down his pipe and picked up the envelope.

It had been almost a week ago since the ship had gone down. The newspaper's front pages were full of the horror and the atrocious estimated death totals. Mr. Ledger had tired of reading the same headlines over and over, so he had refrained from reading the paper this morning.

In the silence, Mr. Ledger ripped open the envelope, wondering who it could be from. The penmanship looked strangely familiar.

*April 15, 1912*

*My dear father,*
*I can only hope and pray that this letter will find its way to*
*your hand. I want to beg for your forgiveness, and beseech*
*you to once again acknowledge me as your son. I've always*
*wanted to make you proud and to bear our family name with*
*honor.*

*I do not believe I will make it home. My ship, the glorious*
*TITANIC, has struck an iceberg and is sinking in the middle*
*of the Atlantic at this very moment as I write to you.*

*Nevertheless, know that I have upheld my duty and that I*
*love you, father. All I ever wanted was to please you.*

*Your son,*
*Damon Ledger*

Mr. Ledger felt his face grow stiff.

His son Damon—on the TITANIC? Now as he
thought about it, he recalled his daughter telling him
that Damon had gone to sea. But Mr. Ledger hadn't
been interested in hearing and had stopped her from
telling him more.

"Shirley, bring me that paper!" Mr. Ledger demanded, desperation suddenly engulfing him.

Shirley hurried in with the newspaper, wondering
what had upset the master.

Mr. Ledger quickly went through the pages, looking under the long columns of names of the survivors.
When he didn't find what he wanted, he reluctantly

looked under the "Lost" column. There he found it.
In bold black letters: **LOST....DAMON LEDGER.**

With a terrible fit of anger and pain, Mr. Ledger
ripped the paper in half and hurled it across the room,
his arm upsetting the lamp on the table. Falling to the
floor, it shattered.

The old man bent over in his chair and wept.